BEHIND THE DARKNESS

AYA SHAMIRI

ISBN 979-888555110-6

Chapter I

ONE

"Daddy," she says it kindly with great love and smile that is full of life, "its eating time!" Her poor dad opens his cumbersome eyes but not because of his fragile and tenuous strength but because of that power that is created by the veracious love and the whole-hearted connection between him and his belle daughter, Amelia. This connection and love is like a benignant dictionary that translates her dad's eagerly speaking eyes' unseen words into clear and visible words!

"Daddy, I know how much hard this will be, but you will have to try opening your mouth; my lovely dad, help me to make your motionless body get better." His watching eyes look at his daughter's beautiful and cheerful face that is the source of tranquility to him; he opens his tightly locked mouth with massive and tremendous capacity that could be used just to raise a pencil. She smiles to him. An affectionate smile that is full of life and tenderness. She inserts the enormously light soup into his mouth with the specialized medical spoon; part of the soup succeeds at escaping the inner and dull cave as it gets all over his neck. But the other part of the soup capitulates and enters his body that contains those desperate organs. Amelia kisses her father's forehead gently as he gets charged with more support and hope so he opens his mouth more for her to feed him better. He looks at her, focuses deep into her eyes, and that strapping connection translates his deep ideas into words for Amelia to understand. "OH OKAY I WILL GET IT NOW!" After she gets the catheter, she inserts it into his bladder excellently to drain the imprisoned urine out of his sick body.

She looks at her watch as she yells: "OH MY GOD! I AM LATE FOR WORK!" She kisses her dad and hurries to her workplace. When she enters the hospital, she gets shocked as she sees all her co-workers, some of them that she knows well but the others not, joined for a discussion. She reaches them with a mocker smile and laugh. – "Good morning late lady, what makes you laugh at us?" –"What is funny Doctor Amelia?" –"Can't you see that we are discussing a serious topic?" "Seeing you all," She says it sarcastically while pointing at them roundly, "together agreeing on the same topic without childish fighting is so normal!" One of those workers grabs her and says sadly, "There is a patient that is in a very tragic condition!" –"An ashamed and diffident body that forgot to hold on its arms and legs that have been amputated!" –"She said that it was a big dangerous accident but..." –"But that's not true because the places were these arms and legs were chopped off from shows clearly that it wasn't because of a burn from hydrochloric acid!" The mockery and childishness smile escapes her face from the terrifying conversation! –"GUYS DID YOU NOTICE SOMETHING WHEN SHE WAS SPEAKING HER STRAINED AND INCOMPREHENSIBLE WORDS?" –"Yes, her palate that is supposed to be a complete roof of her mouth was severed!" –"There is something...." –"That happened to her; something that we are ignorant of!" Amelia asks a question; not her this time, it's the lagging curiosity inside her that asks without her interfere! "Where is she now?" –"She is in the specialized room for the disabilities!" While Amelia thrashes her strong feelings of fear from the hidden frightening image of that oppressed patient, moronic curiosity, and inward sadness, she asks with full pity, "Does she...," the powerful and inward sadness rises greatly in her to dread her and affects her tone of speaking with victory, "...does she has a family?" –"No, she is alone!" –"Such a strange patient; she also said that she would not like anyone to enter her room!" "Do you think it is because of the horrifying and shameful condition she is in?" –"Definitely, Amelia" –"Anyways, such a great hospital has to preserve its eminent reputation. Obviously, our humanitarian hospital administrator would not refuse her demand as respect for her privacy." In a bullish and rosy tone, Amelia replies, "Yes! If we all stand together with our administrator and pray for her then she will obviously flee out of her dark and oppressing state!" –"What about her obsolete body? Will she escape from it too?" Amelia looks blindly at Doctor George after he finished his tumultuous words, but this time the inward and merciless sadness in her strengthens much more than before; it starts killing her hope strenuously and starts to torture her turbulently directly after! But that soulful and aged voice distracts that insane monster from eating her living organs severely!

-"Rest time is over; please everyone go back to work. Doctor Amelia, did anything go wrong since you were late?" –"No Sir, everything is good, and I will go now to my office!" Their sir, Mister Grayson Anthony replies with a pure and likeable smile, –"Great, thank you Miss Amelia for your cooperation dear!"

After several hours passed, Amelia finally finishes her tiring work and rushes to her vulnerable dad.

She opens the door speedily, runs to him longing and says, "Daddy I miss you so much!" She hugs him with all tenderness, but tears are not able to escape to not affect her dad's smiley eyes. "Let me wash you now!" She slowly with full caution takes her poor dad's clothes off, gets his specialized shower equipments, and moves him to the side by side shower basement lovingly with all the power that is supplied by two sources: first, the love connection between them and second, the kind empathy that mourns in her while watching her dad's state and condition through her eyes! She washes her dad like how a mom washes her first baby's body; she dries and covers his body with the soft towel, moves him back to bed, massages his inoperative body for one whole hour, dresses him up, and finally, she looks at his elated and pleased eyes like how a mom sees her little son joyous after she dresses him his favorite pajamas. After she feeds him and hydrates his unexpressive body with water, she kisses his forehead and gets him back to sleep. Sleeping is the best sad method to avoid this…THIS FEROCIOUS AND AWFUL REALISM OF THIS SAVAGE LIFE!

Chapter II

TWO

The sun shines; its glowing rays awaken **every** living body smoothly.

Amelia gets up quickly, **wakes up her dad** to give him the required medicine, feeds him, and gets him back to sprawl. She can now go to work with the peaceful serenity that is welcomed by her brain. As she enters the hospital, her hypocritical brain traumatizes that serenity by switching on the recorded distressing event! She works really hard again and repeatedly not for her dad's iniquitous body but for that maltreated yet bonny soul in it!

After long hours of work, she hurries to get out of her workplace until she gets hit by the still and motionless nurse. "I am so sorry... Miss Samantha is there anything wrong?" Samantha turns to face Amelia with her aroused brain and says sadly, -"That patient is in real danger; her weary face was so exhausted ..." "OH GOD! WE SHOULD RUSH TO HELP HER!" -"No, As I entered the room she was in to help Mr. Anthony quickly prepare the defibrillators, she started acting insanely and grisly, so I left with fear that was blinding my eyes. But that scene of her tiresome face was strong enough to beat this fear to allow my eyes to see it clearly!"

- "SHE WOULD DIE RATHER THAN TO BE SEEN IN HER CONDITION!" -"Anyways, don't worry, she is monitored all time, and Mr. Anthony checks on her repeatedly in case of any problem." She directly then remembers her own patient who is waiting at home and runs to him.

As she reaches her home, she runs to her dad and directly starts to feed him. She takes off his shirt, puts cream on his timeworn back, and massages it with her soft and velvet hands. She then puts on his beseeching shirt that screams out loud for salvage, returns him to bed, and finally kisses his deceased and old hands! She reads the words, "I am so blessed for having such an affectionate and wonderful daughter like you! I love you my little daughter!" not from a page neither from a message, but from that magical and incorporeal dictionary that translates his eyes' terms. –"Dad, do you want to hear a story?" His eyes smile with gladness.

"That Cage" She starts telling the story, but there is something... something in her... a voice... a great voice inside her that whispers and exhorts someone... Who is this someone...? Why will this mysterious voice alert that unknown... and from what?

"A family that consists of: a dad, a mom, a son, and a baby. The unavailable dad is in another and far country, the mom who does her arduous daily house routine lives with her son and baby. The son is successful in his life but that baby... that baby is caged... caged in a loathsome and tight cage that is full of blackness!" She speaks with deep and meaning full sadness, "Now dad, you might ask yourself that why the mom does not rescue her baby!" "The mom cannot rescue her little innocent baby because she is unable to do that; that cage is the most sturdy and tough cage in the universe. This mom is capable of doing one thing only which is **watching her little wronged and charming baby dying gradually in front of her dejected eyes inside that merciless beast.**" She stops as she sees her dad's eyes crying emotionally; she hugs him tightly with all love combined with warm-heartedness feelings. She says while crying severely with pain that anguishes her inside, "Dad! DAD! YOU UNDERSTOOD.... DIDN'T YOU!" She hugs him tighter and says, "I am so sorry dad! I just want to show you...," she points to her heart while her eyes are fighting to keep her naughty tears under control and continues, "I just want to show you how much I feel what you feel, how much I suffer when you suffer, and how much my inside celebrates happily when you smile!" She sleeps next to her poor dad who wishes to hug her but cannot!

That caged baby is the delightful soul of that paralyzed person that gets imprisoned by the pitiless cage which is his paralyzed body! That mom reflects the doctor who works so hard to take care of those patients but cannot because the accused and unfair life is much greater and stronger! That dad reflects the amount of money that is needed to keep that baby alive

but not for rescuing! That voice inside her was her soul that alerted her dad's soul from hearing this depressive story that reflects the true reality!

Chapter III

THREE

The gloomy sun arises, but the supportive clouds try to distract the cynical in this pessimistic sun by blocking its way!

Amelia gets up and kisses her dad to go to work. As she reaches her work, her quiet steps get disturbed by the fuss that is happening! The fuss of nurses' loud and accelerating steps, the fuss of the numerous words that carry sympathy with it, finally her steps cut off as she hears the most detestable and ruffian noise:

BEEP! BEEP! BEEP! She looks at the source of this cursed noise; she sees Mr. Anthony with his miserable face that had already covered that defeated patient with the shroud! She is dead! As they carry her to the morgue, Amelia complains desperately with her warm and continuous tears, "HOW MUCH, MY LORD, SHOULD WE FEEL SORRY FOR OUR SELVES! MY LORD, OUR CRUSHABLE AND HELPLESS BODIES ARE CALLING FOR YOUR MERCY ON US LIKE HOW A THREE YEAR OLD BABY THAT IS LOST IN A LARGE FORREST, SURROUNDED BY THE WORLD'S MOST VIOLENT LIONS AND WOLVES, AND IN DARK NIGHT CALLS HIS MOM IN A HYSTERIAS WAY! WHY DOES

LIFE ATTRACT US BY HAPPINESS AS A LURE TO DESTROY US INTO TORTURED PIECES!"

She goes to her office blindly to continue working. She has to continue as if nothing had happened because after life steps on our brittle bodies, it moves on!

After long hours of work which at least were helpful to forget that depressive incident, she walks to exit the hospital. She sees one of the workers who is about to lock the mortuary; she runs to him and asks to see that patient, but this is not her who is asking. It is that harmful curiosity in her! He takes her in to the frightening room and leaves her alone.

She walks in towards that patient's morgue! Step by Step! Step by Step! Curiosity... not alone...curiosity combined with suspicious fear that spills out of her body with each step she takes because of the great amount of this unpleasant combination that fills her body more than the maximum! Another step is taken where her quick heartbeats would soon or later shoot out her heart out of her body because it would rather join to those dead bodies than experiencing the coming unknown! She opens the morgue! Her heart wishes to be dead and disabled, her brain wishes to cut off fiercely those jolted and shocked watching eyes!

"MOM!"

Great depression arrives with sturdy darkness that eagerly feed on the girl's **kept** hopes, cheerfulness, and aspiration.

Her sharply shocked and greatly confused eyes observe all the lethal cuts, prickled left eye, and ripped whitish lips on that depleted face that unfortunately should be now referred as her mom's face!

-"Oh! Doctor Amelia, you are still here!" the concussion was still present, but her face forced away her thoughts before the worker notices anything. –"Yes... I am ...st.. still here..." She leaves quickly and walks absentminded; her mind is taken by the thoughts of what she just saw and her eyes are still viewing that hair-raising image of that weary face. When she reaches home, she sees her only source of tranquility. She runs to her dad and hugs him softly without waking him up then she rushes to her room quickly before her knocking tears would flow down; she goes to the bed absentminded, her face sinks into the pillow, and cries soundlessly to not wake up that caged soul.

-"MOM, HOW DID YOU DIE? WHY DID U LEAVE US? WHY DID YOU RUN AWAY FROM US?" She holds her over-weighted head before it falls and murmurs sorrowfully; "I needed you mommy. I needed you mightily! Mightily, Mom..!"

"It is so dark; I am so ignorant of what is happening! My fearful eyes are watching all the darkness that is the reflection of the blankness in my mind." She starts hitting her hurting head over and over again. "OH MY GOD... I HATE THIS DARKNESS!" Her blank brain could do nothing other than forcing her eyes to shut down for sleep.

After the day passes, Amelia opens her eyes but couldn't get up.

The powerful solicitude in her pushed her up to check her mom's old account which contained her pictures. Her eyes are waiting impatiently to see her mom's pictures but... the account was deleted... just recently deleted... before very few minutes.

-"WHAT THE HELL IS THIS! If my mom is dead now then who the hell deleted her account?" She walks to her dad desperately, feeds him, washes his body very well and gently, and helps him wear his clothes when her mind is totally occupied. She hugs him and kisses him with great love so he can get back to sleep comfortably. The harsh conditions forces Amelia to keep on working really hard beyond her ability. Amelia, life's victim, goes to her work and start working really hard for her poor daddy, and for their lives; after she works for several hours and finished her job, she decides to leave home fearfully because of the unknown that might arrive with creepy surprises that life might sometimes gives us.

When she reaches home, she runs to change the catheter for her dad and kisses him tenderly; but suddenly... then suddenly.... She feels a heavy weight on her back that seems like an object is stable on her back in some way. As she turns her head slowly, she notices that this heavy weight is nothing other than her dad's hand! **"DAAAAAAAD! YOU RAISED YOUR HAND...**

AND THIS TIME WITHOUT MY HELP!!!!" Amelia hugs her dad strongly and whispers to herself "You are my whole life, dad! Words are so weak to describe my superior love for you! I love you!" She leaves her dad to rest after she feeds him then runs to her room and sleeps with hopes that are trying to cover the deep scar in her.

Chapter IV

FOUR

The sun arises, and silence is filling the house but gets disturbed suddenly.

*Ring! Ring! Ring!*Amelia answers her phone with a smile that gets torn away suddenly. The river abruptly flows from her pitiful eyes. Her hands quickly lock the eruption inside her by blocking her mouth to not wake up her dad!

-*"My beautiful girl; oh god, how much I love her! Please lord save her, protect her, and make her happy. She is the only one who the sugar cubes will look and taste bitter compared to her charming sweetness. Sometimes she would break everything into pieces but her beautiful features will make me speechless! God prevent her from the evil darkness. I might be blind, maybe not by eyes, but she will always arise like a sunflower greater than a candle power."*

The phone then hangs up leaving Amelia thunderstruck!

"Th... this is .. tha... tha..t song you have always sung it for me, MOM!" "Mom what is happening? I KNOW NOTHING! I AM LOCKED IN THIS DARKNESS OF *IGNORANCE!*" She falls sadly on the floor bringing the phone closer to her heart and cries sorrowfully!

Amelia decides to go search about any clues of what happened to her mom in the places she visited in the past.

"Where shall I search first??" Her mind turns on the old videotape that contains memories from the past!

-"Mommy, why don't you work with my dad?" –"Destiny chooses for us our place of sustenance and not us! It chose for me a far place to work in." –"It's the Fabulous Store!" Her mom looks at her little daughter with a surprised face. "My dad refuses to take me there since it is the farthest place from here!" –"Wow, My clever sweetheart knew where I work without I tell her!"

"Okay then, I will start my journey from that store!" She walks slowly without waking up her dad and leaves the house for the search.

After few hours, she reached to the Fabulous Store that was still opened, and this drew a big smile on her face. She enters the store nervously and starts to buy few groceries just to ignore any awkward situations; as she looks at the ground, she tells herself with great nostalgia that brings some tears to her eyes "I cannot believe it! I can't believe that I am stepping on the floor that my mom stepped on! I can't believe that I am in the place that my mom was present in! I can't bel…………" –"Oh dear are you okay? Didn't you see the box infront of you before you fall?" –"I am fine! My back just hurts a little bit."

The lady worker starts laughing and asks her for her name then Amelia replies friendly and decides to ask her the question she came for!

–"Can I ask you about a person who worked here before several years ago?" –"Look my grandma has the list of all the workers who worked here long time ago because she thinks their names are valuable enough to be kept rather than forgotten. –"You're Grandma!" "Yes! Yes! She is the owner of this shop; she got old so I am taking care now!" Miss Sandra grabs Amelia's hand, goes to the next by house, and knocks. An old woman opens and welcomes them with a heartwarming smile saying "Please come in!" –"HI GRANDMA!" –"Hi dear!" –"My friend wants to ask you about an old worker who used to work in our shop." –"Yes obviously, just tell me the name dear!" –" Codica" the grandma stops looking through the papers as she hears that name and her face turns red with great anger! –"GET OUT OF MY HOUSE RIGHT NOW!" –"But what did she do! Please tell me! I beg you!" "GET OUT OF MY HOUSE RIGHT NOW!!!" Amelia cries and as she steps out –"Codica Phillips stole me and my shop so I kicked her out!" Amelia inhales deeply with great relieve and says politely, "Codica Jerson Christopher that is my mom!" _"Oh dear, I am so sorry for what I just did and this name never crossed my shop." "It is totally fine, and I understand; have a good day." Amelia leaves the house desperately and all hopes are crushed! Her mom lied to her!

As she reaches her home, she throws her bag, runs to feed her dad, and does a massage for him until he sleeps well. She gets back to her bed; as she is almost about to close her eyes for a sleep, the sound of receiving a notification woke her. She opens the message and reads the following sentence:

"You are my precious treasure!"

Amelia starts crying hysterically; she gets up on her bed and starts to pull her hair strongly. She slaps her face again and again! Why shall life hurt people to an extent that they start losing their minds? Why does life suck all our hopes and happiness from us? We are so weak and vulnerable! The tired mind gets up and turns on the other old video tape.

-"Mommy, I want to tell you something but please don't be mad at me!" –"Yes honey, tell me." –"When you and daddy were at work, someone knocked the door so I thought it was you because you forgot your keys..." –"Don't tell me you opened for a stranger, Amelia!" –"I did, and then I noticed it was a strange man so I directly locked the door!" –"Well, I have a great idea; let us create a secret sentence!" –"A secret sentence!" –"Whenever someone knocks the door, the secret sentence will have to be said." –"What will be our secret code mom?" –"You are my precious treasure!" The little girl goes and hugs her mom tightly!"

The day passed with great difficulty.

Amelia washes her dad and feeds him his favorite soup. She tells her dad a lot of stories and then tells him a joke that made him smile cheerfully. That meant the world to Amelia! She hugs her dad as all her tears fall off, and he hugs her too. Life is so dirty compared to such a pure and truthful love!!!!

After Amelia returns back from her work, she runs to check on her sleeping dad. She then goes to her room, but she gets disturbed by a phone call! This time she is shivering to answer, but she will.

"Hello! Who is with me?" –"That ignorant skull knew the insignificance of that crown!" –"WHO THE HELL AR..." The phone hangs up! She calls that number again with a fatal anger! "WHO ARE YOU?" –"You will regret calling this number back." –"SHUT YOUR MOUTH UP AND TE...." Noises!! She hears noises! But these noises are abnormal! They sound like... like horrifying screaming that resulted from killing torture... no... no... Even worse!

"MOM! WHY ARE YOU SCREAMING? MOM!" –"I can hear the shaking noises of your freaked out organs that might jump out of you any moment!" The phone hangs up!

"MOM! SHE IS DEAD! I SAW HER DEAD BODY! THEN WHAT WAS THAT?" She sits and says, "It seems this merciless life will never stop raping me." She weeps melancholically!

The worst darkness a person might face is the darkness of ignorance!

Chapter V

FIVE

After the sun shines the next day, Amelia kisses her dad and runs to her work, and she returns back home exhausted after the long and continues hours of work. The love and caring in her towards her dad erase her exhaustion and make her feel strong all time! As she enters the house, she runs to her dad and puts her head on his chest. Tranquility flows to all her body and head that is full of blindness.

-"Dad! I love you so much!" –"I.. Luf.. yo..." –"DAD!" Amelia cries, and this time she cries from great happiness; her dad gets better with time! This happy incident injected hopes to Amelia. She receives another one! Another call! She looks at her phone with courage as if nothing would dare to ruin the happiness in her! She walks to the other room and answers calmly.

"Yes?" –**"You have two choices; one: continue your life as it is. Continue your life with that wild darkness that feeds on your mind. Two: be courageous enough to see what is behind the darkness. Tomorrow, Memorial Park at 4:00 AM!"** She is so confused and silent! The confusion was powerful enough to block her ability to respond in any way! An insane laugh arises from the phone. The phone hangs up!

Her mind exhaustedly searches in between the old videotapes and turns one of them on.

-"Dear, go get me my shoes fast!" –"offffffffffft! Fine!" Little Amelia walks frustrated and gives her mom the shoes she asked for. –"Here, take it." Her mom knees down towards her daughter. –"Why is my little girl angry?" Amelia looks at her from the side of her eyes and says, "I am so bored; I get to do nothing because you and dad are always at work." –"Go change your clothes and wear your shoes quickly!" –"Why mo..." –"Hurry up!" Amelia rushes to exchange her clothes and wear her shoes as if she is racing time. –"Here I am ready!" She grabs her daughter and closes the house door behind her; at their way to the car, Amelia asks her mom to where they are going, but her mom keeps on being silent. –"Get into the car fast and don't forget to put on the seat belt." –"Okay, mommy!"

After several minutes, they reached.

"Wake up, sweetheart; we reached." –"Mem... Ummm... Memo.." –"Memorial Park, so this is the place I go to when I feel sad or bored. It's refreshing birds' sounds, flowers, and mind-blowing views make me feel like a newborn baby!" –"Is there ice-cream in there?" –"Yes, ice-cream and cotton candy too."Amelia jumps from happiness. Her mom takes her to the park as she keeps on running around excitedly.

"I was happy." She says it again in a more heart touching tone, "I was really happy." Her eyes drop few, heavy, and warm tears that could burn her face!

"Rest in peace, mom" She exhales and inhales deeply... deeply with powerful pain that eats her heart slowly! She shuts her eyes.

BUZZ! BUZZ! BUZZ! BUZZ! Amelia gets up forcedly and runs to see her dad.

After she kisses him tenderly, she washes his weak and heavy body very well, helps him to wear his clothes, feeds him, and hugs him tightly with all love until he falls asleep. Amelia whispers to herself as she looks at her watch, "It is 3:20 AM and I have to leave." She runs to the door after she prepares herself, but there is something that attracted her face towards her dad like a magnet... a very strong magnet indeed. She rushes to her dad to kiss him gently and leaves her home.

Chapter VI

SIX

She arrives to the Memorial Park.

As she steps into the park, she gets dizzy from how much crowded her mind is; numerous thoughts of that anonymous person and the memories of her mom cause that squeeze in her mind! The atmosphere in her head is totally contradicting to the atmosphere around her; it is so quiet and peaceful with almost no people. She looks at her watch nervously when she notices it is 4:00 AM.

She sits on the cold grass alone; she moves her overloaded head to her hands and falls asleep.

Crunch! Crunch! Crunch! Crunch! Crunch! Amelia opens her eyes gradually to see who is approaching her. Her eyes close, but she opens them again. She sees an enormous person standing in front of her! She looks into the face as she sees nothing other than a proficiently hidden identity. An identity that is perfectly hidden behind that huge, black glasses', that large coat that hides the whole body with the neck, that wide mask that is big enough to cover the rest of the face and finally, that hat that envelopes the entire head not leaving even the ears alone.

She gets up quickly as she starts to tremble from fear.

-**"How did your dad get paralyzed?"**

Amelia gets dismayed! She gets shocked enough that her tongue feels so heavy to move. She aghast to an extent that her trembling words refuse to go out strictly. No response!

-**"How did your dad get paralyzed?"**

Amelia is still silent. Who are you? How do you know about my dad? What is your business? All these questions were too many for her exhausted mind to handle! It was all in her head!

Her lackluster eyes come in contact with his large glasses that act like a barrier which doesn't allow her eyes to see and reach this unknown's eyes.

That dark moment came across to Amelia's mind.

While Amelia walks in her high school with her classmates happily, she receives a phone call. "Hi mommy!" –"AMELIA, COME HOME RIGHT NOW!" "Mom! What happened! You know I have a class; don't you?" –'Am.. Amelia.. Your dad..." Her mom's terrifying tone scares her! "MOM! MOM! WHAT IS WRONG WITH MY DAD!" Her mom cries on the phone and tells her that she needs her. "ALRIGHT, MOM! I AM COMING NOW!" When Amelia arrives, she directly throws her bag and runs to her dad. As she sees the doctor calming down her crying mom, she asks confusedly and insanely about her dad. "MOM!

MOM! MO.." –"*Calm down, Amelia... be hopeful he will be fine!*" *Amelia points at her severely pained dad.* "*WHAT HAPPENED TO MY DAD? MOM!*" –"*He fell... he fell!*" *Codica continues crying and says, " from the stairs.... and his ...spinal cord ...got strongly damaged!*" *Amelia's face expresses nothing other than a shock combined with fear for her dad.* "*WHAT WILL HAPPEN TO MY DAD!*" –"*Honey! Your dad...*" "*YOUR DAD WHAT MOM? WHAT? SPEAK!*" –"*Your dad will not move again!*" *Amelia falls on the floor with shock and yells in a hysterious manner for how much she feels sorry for her dad and for how much she loves him!*

She replies frightfully to that anonymous person in front of her.

"**He fell. The fall was strong enough to make him get paralyzed.**"

-"**Arsenic Poison**"

"**What?**"

-"**That's the poison your mom poisoned your dad with.**"

Amelia, the speechless girl, drops on the floor deadly and tries to convince herself that it is all just a prank from one of her stupid friends or coworkers, but the fact that she did not tell anyone on this earth evilly denies that.

-"**It is strong enough to damage the spinal cord which creates a falling effect. That's how your mom paralyzed you dad.**"

She shouts madly. "**WHY THE HELL SHALL I BELIEVE YOU!**"

-**"Fabulous Store, the place your mom pretended to work at."** This unknown expands his arms as if he will say a speech and says calmly, **"when you where thinking that she was working for a very long period of time to help your living, she was with me. The whole time just with me!"**

Amelia's mind and thoughts leave her blank and escape this stressful surrounding!

This anonymous person comes closer to Amelia who is terrified and shocked from what is happening. Closer.... Closer.... Closer... few centimeters are between them. This person gets out a large and very sharp chainsaw that looks so dirty!

Thank you god for giving Amelia's poor body enough support for her to move backward.

"Don't kill me! I beg you! Don't kill me!" While he is approaching her, she cries exhaustedly and says, **"I have to take care of my dad! Don't kill me! I want to stay for him!".**

-**"Do not worry dear! I will not kill you."** He drops that chainsaw exactly next to her. **"I just wanted you to see with what you mom was severely tortured."**

"NO WAY! NO WAY! YOU TORTURED MY MOM!"

-**"Yes, I got your dad's revenge.... I forced her to taste that poison too."**

She cries harder and harder. She is totally vulnerable!

-**"But I ended her at the end! I finished her from all that torturing. See I am a good person.**

I am not that bad as you think!"

Poor Amelia covers her ears fast. **"SHUT UP!"**

-**"Your mom and I loved each other to death that is why I told her to pretend working in the furthest store just to spend more time with me."**

Silence locks Amelia's expressions and responses.

-**"We love each other to death; the thought that blinded me from the evil reality! That dark and revealing moment unfortunately arriv..."**

"ENOUGH!" she screams louder and louder; her loud voice sucks all her energy that leaves her body squashed. **"NO MORE PLEASE!"**

-**"Until that moment arrived. I heard her telling her friend that she faked her love for me ....you know why? "** Madly, he approaches closer to her face.He screams insanely when he hits his chest hard. **"BECAUSE OF MONEYYYY! SHE LOVED MY POCKET AND NOT ME!"**

"STOP!" she starts slapping her face as she screams. **"STOP IT! ENOUGH! ENOUGH! ENOUGH YOU... YOU UGLY DEVIL!"**

-**"She betrayed me! She betrayed you! She betrayed your dad! SEE SHE DESERVED ALL THAT! I am not bad, see."**

He gets closer to her and lifts her up gently!

-**"I am not bad!"**

Amelia takes her phone quickly. As she presses on 91.., he snatches the phone from her.

-**"I already did-"**

She looks at him amazed that he called the police to arrest himself.

-"**Before I get executed, I would like to give you a gift.**"

He handles a paper. She takes it when her heart pumps so fast! Her mind still did not return back! She opens the message. Don't read it, Amelia. Don't read it!

WAAAAAAAAAHHHH !WAAAAAAAAAHHH! WAAAAAAAAAHHHH !WAAAAAAAAAHHH! WAAAAAAAAAHHHH !WAAAAAAAAAHHH!

The police car noises were not strong enough to distract her from reading that paper.

She reads the following:

The alleged father is not excluded as the biological father of the tested child. Based on the testing results obtained from the analysis of DNA loci listed, the probability of paternity is 99.9998%. It is medically proven that Amelia is the biological daughter of Mr. GRAYSON ANTHONY.

He reveals his face and identity. Amelia slowly raises her head from the paper towards his face. Her administrator, this unknown person, and her mom's killer was the whole time her real father!

Shock sticks her face in place not allowing it to move in any way. It is so NOISY!

-"**ARREST HIM NOW!**"

-"**MISS! ARE YOU OKAY!**"

-"**MISS!**" **DID HE HURT YOU? MISS! MISS! MISS!**"

All lights blear and clash into each other! All sounds get louder and louder battling each other ! All in her head... Until suddenly... nothing!!

-"*My beautiful girl; oh god, how much I love her! Please lord save her, protect her, and make her happy. She is the only one who the sugar cubes will look and taste bitter compared to her charming sweetness. Sometimes she would break everything into pieces but her beautiful features will make me speechless! God prevent her from the evil darkness. I might be blind, maybe not by eyes, but she will always arise like a sunflower greater than a candle power.*"

"*Mommy I love you so much! Your voice makes me feel so sleepy and safe.*"

–"*My dear little daughter, sleep and I will always forever as long as I live, I will never stop singing for you.*"

THE END

About The Author

Aya Wajih Shamiri was a student in tenth grade at Saud International School which she was raised in with all love and with great educational support when she wrote this book. Aya is from Yemen as her country means the world to her, however, she lives now in Saudi Arabia since it's much safer. Her parents were and will always be the first and main source of support to her. Perihan Tokaishem, her best friend who provided her with some help as she also fills the gap in Aya's heart of not having any sisters.

www.ingramcontent.com/pod-product-compliance
Lightning Source LLC
Chambersburg PA
CBHW031430160726
47993CB00003B/1488